POKÉMON
THE JOHTO JOURNEYS

Prize Pokémon

Adapted by Sheila Sweeny

SCHOLASTIC INC.
New York   Toronto   London   Auckland   Sydney
Mexico City   New Delhi   Hong Kong   Buenos Aires

JOHTO REGION

No part of this book may be reproduced, stored in a retrieval system, or transmitted in any form or by any means, electronic, mechanical, photocopying, recording, or otherwise, without written permission of the publisher. For information regarding permission, write to Scholastic Inc., Attention: Permissions Department, 555 Broadway, New York, NY 10012.

ISBN 0-439-20276-0

© 1995–2001 Nintendo, CREATURES, GAME FREAK.
TM & ® are trademarks of Nintendo.

Copyright © 2001 Nintendo.
All rights reserved. Published by Scholastic Inc.
SCHOLASTIC and associated logos are trademarks
and/or registered trademarks of Scholastic Inc.

12 11 10   12 13 14 15 16/0

Printed in the U.S.A.
First Scholastic printing, October 2001

The Sad Sunflora

Ash Ketchum plodded down the road. He didn't have the energy to stand up straight. Ash was hot and tired, but most of all he was thirsty. Pikachu, his Electric Pokémon, was thirsty, too. Beads of sweat poured down its face. Pikachu looked like it was ready to collapse.

Ash's friend Misty shook her canteen. "This canteen is dry as a bone," she said.

Togepi, Misty's eggshell Pokémon, peered into the empty canteen. *"Togi togi,"* it said sadly.

Ash looked to his friend Brock. "How far is it to the next town?" he asked.

Ash, Misty, and Brock were exploring the Johto Region. While they were here, Ash hoped to catch some new Pokémon and earn badges by battling Johto gym leaders.

Ash had even heard that there were special Pokémon festivals in the Johto Region. He was anxious to see if that were true.

Brock looked in his guidebook and answered Ash, "Well, according to this, we're not far from a place called Bloomingvale."

"How far is 'not far'?" Ash wisecracked. Then Ash spotted water spurting from a pipe lying on the ground.

"Is that real, or is it a mirage?" Misty wondered.

It was the real thing, all right. Ash approached a young girl who was working on the pipe. She had two dark pigtails and a straw hat to shade her face from the hot sun.

"Excuse me, miss," Ash rasped. "Is it okay if we take a drink from that pipe?"

The girl happily let Ash and his friends have a drink.

"This is super-nice of you," Misty said thankfully as she introduced herself.

"No problem," replied the girl with a smile. "My name is Sonrisa. It's nice to meet you."

Ash and his friends watched as Sonrisa fixed the broken pipe. Then she led the friends to her hometown, Bloomingvale. Ash, Misty, and Brock looked around at the beautiful green plants and trees that lined the streets of the town.

"Bloomingvale seems really nice," Ash commented.

"I love it," Sonrisa said cheerfully. "The sun shines almost every single day! The

weather's perfect for raising my favorite Pokémon."

Ash was curious to find out what Sonrisa's Pokémon might be. He eagerly followed Sonrisa to her house. There was a greenhouse next door. Sonrisa turned on a sprinkler system. Water squirted all over the green lawn.

"Okay, time for your daily sprinkle," Sonrisa shouted.

The greenhouse door opened, and several Pokémon came running out. Ash had never seen anything like them. They had long green bodies, with leaf-shaped arms and legs. Their round smiling faces were surrounded by yellow petals. The Pokémon danced around happily under the water spray.

"Are those Sunflora?" asked Brock.

"Yes. There a lot of them here in town," replied Sonrisa. "In fact, Bloomingvale is famous for Sunflora."

Ash consulted Dexter, his Pokédex. Dexter was a palm-sized computer that held information about all of the world's Pokémon.

"Sunflora, the Sun Pokémon," said Dexter. "This smiling

Pokémon loves the sun, but it also needs plenty of water to grow and stay healthy."

"Pure water makes the Sunflora happy," Sonrisa said. "And they have to be happy or they don't have a chance at the Sunflora Festival."

"Sunflora Festival?" Ash asked. "What's that?"

Sonrisa explained that Sunflora trainers in Bloomingvale worked hard all year long to get their Sunflora ready for the annual festival. Each trainer could enter one Sunflora in the festival. Judges selected one sun Pokémon to be named Sunflora of the Year. Sonrisa had never won first place, but she thought she might have a chance this year.

"How are you doing, Sonrisa?" came a booming voice from down the street. It was Cyrus, Sonrisa's big, red-haired neighbor. Cyrus had won the Sunflora of the Year award three times.

"Why aren't you training your Sunflora?" Cyrus asked Sonrisa.

"We did some training earlier and now I'm just watering them," Sonrisa answered.

"Well, I hope it makes them happy," Cyrus chuckled. "I just heard that Lester's doing something to make his Sunflora even happier. He's hired a comedian. Now that's a laugh!"

"It sounds like the trainers around here are pretty desperate to win," noted Misty.

Sonrisa pointed to a trainer down the street. The girl and her Sunflora both had golden brown faces. "She takes her Sunflora to a tanning salon," Sonrisa said. "And the trainer there works with his Sunflora to build up its strength." Ash saw that a boy was making his Sunflora haul a tire up and down a driveway.

"Do you do anything special to train your Pokémon, Sonrisa?" asked Brock.

"I just give them fresh air, clean water, and try to keep them happy!" answered Sonrisa.

Ash looked at Sonrisa's Sunflora. They all had happy, smiling faces. All but one, that is. It seemed rather glum.

"It looks like this one has a problem," Ash remarked.

Sonrisa frowned. "That's my prize Sunflora, Sonny. I was going to enter it in the

competition," Sonrisa said, "but lately it's been so sad!"

"Hey, why don't you try to let us cheer it up for you?" Brock suggested.

"Sure," Ash agreed. "You helped us out. We can help make your Sunflora smile again."

"Do you really think you can do it?" Sonrisa asked. "Sonny hasn't smiled for days."

Ash grinned. He loved a challenge. "Don't worry, Sonrisa," Ash said. "Your Sunflora will win first prize, or my name isn't Ash Ketchum!"

2

Meowth's Bad Luck

Brock got to work right away. He stuck out his tongue. He made funny faces at the Sunflora. The Sunflora didn't even grin.

Pikachu tried next. *"Pika pika,"* squeaked Pikachu as it danced around in front of the Sunflora. Even the sight of the cute little yellow Pokémon didn't cheer up the sun Pokémon.

The sun was setting behind the purple mountains that surrounded Bloomingvale. Suddenly, all of the Sunflora headed back into the greenhouse.

"What's happening?" Ash asked.

"They're just getting ready for the sun to set," Sonrisa told Ash. "Sunflora go to sleep as soon as the sun goes down!"

"*Sunflora, sunflora,*" the Sunflora chimed in.

"We're going to have to find a place for *our* beauty sleep," joked Ash. "Is there a Poké-mon Center nearby?" Ash knew that most towns had a Pokémon Center where trainers and their Pokémon could get food and rest.

Sonrisa directed them to the Blooming-

vale Pokémon Center, which was right down the street.

"See you in the morning, Sonrisa," Ash said as they walked away. "We'll be back tomorrow to make Sunflora smile."

Later, as Ash, Brock, and Misty slept at the Pokémon Center, two heads peeked out from behind a tree near the greenhouse. One belonged to a girl with long red hair. The other was a boy with purple hair. They were Jessie and James — and the talking Pokémon, Meowth, wasn't far behind them. Team Rocket was brewing trouble again!

James picked the lock on the front door of the greenhouse. Soon, Team Rocket was inside.

"Look at this!" marveled Meowth. "There's got to be a zillion Sunflora in here!"

The Sunflora were all sleeping peacefully. Each Sunflora's head drooped down to face the floor.

Jessie and James wanted to steal all the Sunflora and sell them. But Meowth had a different idea.

"We're going to enter the Sunflora contest!" Meowth told Jessie and James.

"Why in the world would we do that?" Jessie snapped.

"No reason," replied Meowth. "Except that the grand prize is a year's supply of instant noodles!"

Meowth rubbed its stomach. Team Rocket might have been famous Pokémon thieves, but they weren't very good at it. That meant they were usually broke — and hungry.

Jessie licked her lips. "It would be like winning the instant lottery — only with noodles," she said. "We've got to find a Sunflora that can win that contest!"

Meowth took out a device that looked like a flashlight.

"I've got just the thing to help us find a winner." Meowth purred. "A sunlight simulator!"

Meowth turned on the device. Bright light shone on all the Sunflora. The Sunflora were tricked. They thought it was daytime. They raised their heads and smiled.

Soon the greenhouse was filled with the sound of Sunflora chattering, *"Sunflora! Flora, flora!"*

"Is it just me or do all these sappy, smiling Sunflora look the same?" grumbled Jessie.

"Jessie, each one of these Sunflora is unique!" instructed James.

He looked around at each Sunflora. He found a flaw in every one. One didn't have the right shape. One lacked personality. One had an insincere smile. One just didn't want to win badly enough.

Jessie studied each Sunflora, too. They still all looked the same to her. Meowth was acting silly and dancing around, excited at the thought of all those noodles. Then Meowth's paw clumsily bumped into a red button.

"Hey, that button just ran into my paw!" Meowth howled.

An alarm shrieked. A net fell from the ceiling. It landed right on Meowth!

"Run for it!" shouted James.

"Where are you going?" hissed Meowth.

Jessie and James bolted out of the greenhouse door. They ran so fast they left a trail of dust clouds behind them. They also left Meowth all tied up back in the greenhouse. Team Rocket had really brewed up some trouble this time, and Meowth was caught right in the middle of it!

3

Together Again

Ash woke up from his sleep to hear Cyrus shouting.

"Come back here you thieves!" he yelled angrily.

Cyrus's cries woke the others, too. They ran to the greenhouse to see what had happened.

"A bell went off in the greenhouse," Cyrus explained. "When I came out to check it, I caught this cat burglar!"

"It's Meowth!" Ash, Misty, and Brock shouted all at once.

"I can't believe Jessie and James just left me here like I was yesterday's kitty litter," Meowth screeched.

Ash stared at the white, scratch cat Pokémon. Cyrus had taken Meowth from the net and tied a rope around its body.

Seeing Meowth caught like this gave Misty an idea. She leaned over and whispered a plan into Ash's ear.

"Let's go for it!" Ash said.

Misty turned to Cyrus. "I beg your pardon," she said politely. "We have a feeling

this Pokémon is just an innocent victim. It must have been corrupted by the two who ran away!"

Meowth looked shocked that Misty was trying to help.

"If you let us have it we'll make sure it stays out of trouble," Misty added.

"Well, since it didn't actually steal anything, I guess it's okay," Cyrus agreed.

Misty pulled Meowth by the rope around its neck.

"Now come along!" Misty ordered Meowth.

"Wow! Wait till Jessie and James hear the twerps sprung me," mewed a surprised Meowth. "You three losers aren't so bad after all!"

Ash, Misty and Brock brought Meowth to Sonrisa. Misty explained her plan. Meowth understood Pokémon language. Meowth could talk to Sonrisa's Sunflora. The Sunflora could tell Meowth why it was feeling so sad.

"Now Meowth can finally use that big mouth for something good!" Ash joked.

Sonrisa brought Sonny out from the greenhouse. Pikachu and Togepi watched with interest to see what Meowth would learn.

"What's up, smiley?" Meowth asked the Sunflora. "You're looking even more like a sourpuss than me!"

"*Sunflora. Flora, flora. Sunflora,*" chirped Sonny.

"Sunflora is sad," Meowth translated. "It misses another Sunflora it used to play with."

"What little friend are you talking about, Sonny?" asked Misty.

"*Flora flora,*" answered the Sunflora.

"It says it was a Sunflora that belonged to the kid who lives down the street," explained Meowth.

Sonrisa knew who that Sunflora was right away. It belonged to Cyrus.

Just then, a rope lassoed Meowth and dragged it away.

Ash squinted into the darkness. He should have known. Jessie and James had come back to rescue Meowth.

"Thanks for helping us out, Meowth!" Misty laughed as she watched Meowth's head bump along the ground.

"Me-ouch!" howled Meowth.

The friends agreed to meet early in the morning. Sonrisa couldn't wait to talk to Cyrus. He had the key to cheering up Sonny.

"You must mean Grindala," Cyrus told them. "I traded that Sunflora yesterday for one of Nurse Joy's Pokémon."

Luckily, they knew just where to find Nurse Joy. Every town Ash had visited had a Nurse Joy. They all had orange hair, they were all cousins, and they all worked in the town's Pokémon Center.

Nurse Joy knew right away which Pokémon Sonrisa was looking for. When the two Sunflora saw each other again, they danced with joy. They hugged each other tightly.

"Sunflora," said Grindala.

"Sunflora," said Sonny. The Pokémon smiled happily.

"I wish I knew what they were saying," said Ash.

Brock tried to sound like a Sunflora. "I was so sad when you didn't come to the playground," he said. "I thought I'd never see you again."

The friends laughed at Brock's impression.

"It's been so long since I've seen Sonny smile!" said Sonrisa.

Nurse Joy invited Sonrisa and Sonny to visit whenever they wanted.

Sonrisa was glad to see Sonny happy again. But she wondered if it was enough to win the competition.

Ash had another worry on his mind.

What exactly was Team Rocket up to this time?

4

The Heat Is On!

The day of the festival had arrived. Ash, Pikachu, Misty, Brock, and Sonrisa walked around the Sunflora Festival grounds. Misty carried Togepi. The eggshell Pokémon waved its arms at all the sights and sounds. Colorful flags flapped in the wind. Balloons flew everywhere. Ash could hardly resist the smell of fried chicken and hamburgers that were coming from the many food stands.

Near the stage, Bloomingvale trainers lined up to enter the Sunflora contest. Two of the trainers were new to Bloomingvale.

Ash thought their Sunflora looked very strange.

Ash didn't know it, but the new trainers were Jessie and James. Jessie was wearing a dress and high heels. Her hair was up in a bun. James had on a nice shirt, pants, and glasses. It was the perfect disguise. They looked just like the Bloomingvale towns-people. If you looked closely at their Sun-flora, however, you could see little claws sticking out of a taped-up costume. This was no thorny flower. It was Meowth!

"Why am I the one who's wearing this silly Sunflora getup?" Meowth complained.

"Because you're the one who ruined our plan to steal a real Sunflora," said Jessie smugly.

"But my face is all stretched out, my tail is all squished in, and my paws are all messed up!" Meowth whined.

"If you won't do it for us," pleaded James, "at least do it for that year's supply of noo-dles!"

"Okay, I'll try." Meowth sighed.

Ash didn't notice Team Rocket's disguises. He watched as the contestants made their way to the rainbow-colored stage. The judges examined all the Sunflora, and then a voice blared over the loudspeaker.

"Now here are the finalists hoping to be named Sunflora of the Year!" the festival announcer said as he introduced the contestants. The crowd cheered loudly.

"Pika! Pika!" Pikachu joined in. It smiled at the sight of the pretty Sunflora.

"First, here's our returning champion Cyrus and his Sunflora, Dorabelle!"

Cyrus and Dorabelle walked to the center of the stage. Cyrus was big, but Dorabelle was even bigger. In fact, Dorabelle towered over Cyrus! It was the biggest Sunflora in the competition by far.

"It's humongous!" Ash said in amazement.

The announcer spoke again. "Next up is Sonrisa and her Sunflora with the fresh, mountain-spring smile!"

Sonrisa and Sonny walked to the center of the stage. Sonny's smile beamed out to the crowd. No one could tell that just the day before she was the saddest Sunflora in town. Ash, Brock, and Misty cheered as loudly as they could.

"Sonrisa!" Brock shouted.

"Go get 'em!" screamed Ash.

"Pikachu," cheered Pikachu.

Then the announcer told the crowd that there was a last-minute change. Two trainers named Rock and Etta were entering their Sunflora in the contest. Jessie, James, and the disguised Meowth walked to the center of the stage. Jessie and James raised their hands in the air triumphantly.

"Do those two look kind of familiar to you?" Ash asked his friends.

"Yeah," answered Brock.

"So does that Sunflora!" added Misty.

Up on the stage, the judges jotted down their scores. The contestants held their breaths as they waited to hear what the judges had to say.

"The sheer size of Cyrus's Sunflora is simply astounding," noted one judge. "It's very impressive!"

"I think Sonrisa's Sunflora has one of the loveliest smiles I've ever seen!" said another judge.

A third judge agreed. "It's quite clear that either of those two could be named the winner."

"But this third one," said the first judge. "There's something odd about it."

"It looks as though that Sunflora has thorns at the base of its leaves," said the second judge. "It creates a wildflower effect. I quite like it!"

"If it's a new species, then I think it's wonderful," commented the third judge.

If Ash thought the Sunflora looked

strange, something even stranger happened next. Ash saw a little pink Snubbull run up onto the stage. It pounced on the weird-looking Sunflora and bit into its white tail with its sharp teeth. The Sunflora screamed.

Ash almost rushed to help until he realized that the screaming Sunflora was no real Sunflora — it was a Pokémon wearing a costume! Meowth leaped into the air, with Snubbull attached to its tail.

"That's Meowth!" shouted Ash, Misty, and Brock.

Suddenly, the stage was filled with smoke. Jessie and James tore off their outfits to reveal their Team Rocket costumes underneath. They grabbed the microphone from the announcer.

"Prepare for trouble," James laughed.

"Make it double," added Jessie.

Team Rocket shouted their battle cry.

"To protect the world from devastation.

To unite all peoples within our nation.

To denounce the evils of truth and love.

To extend our reach to the stars above.

Jessie!

James!

Team Rocket blast off at the speed of light.

Surrender now or prepare to fight, fight, fight!"

"Meeoooowwwwwtttttthhhh — don't bite!" howled Meowth.

Jessie grabbed the Snubbull and tossed it off the stage. The Snubbull went flying over the crowd and landed safely in the soft grass.

"All right, let's put our plan into action!" shouted Jessie.

"Right," answered James. "This may be the brightest idea we've ever had!"

James worked a remote control. Metal

poles rose up from the tops of the trees that bordered the outdoor judging area. On top of each pole was a giant, shiny panel shaped like a rectangle. The rectangles were actually mirrored sunlight reflectors. Ash had to shield his eyes from the blinding light.

As the sunlight shone on the Sunflora, their heads began to grow. They grew bigger and bigger, until soon they were too big for the Sunflora to hold up. One by one the Sunflora's heads drooped to the ground.

"What's going on?" asked Misty.

"Something terrible!" Ash observed.

The trainers looked on helplessly as their Sunflora struggled to hold up their huge heads.

"When Sunflora get such a strong dose of sunlight, their heads grow so fast that they collapse!" Jessie snickered.

"And they can't use their attacks to get in our way!" sneered James.

Ash knew James was right. The Sunflora were helpless.

"Now Team Rocket's going to steal all of the Sunflora!" Misty cried.

5

A Fight to the Finish

"Wrong as usual, twerps!" taunted Jessie.

"You're not using your noodle!" laughed James.

James used the remote control again. Team Rocket's balloon appeared from behind the trees and hovered over the pile of noodles. A net dropped from the balloon and captured the pile of prizes. Ash realized that Team Rocket didn't want to steal the Sunflora at all. They were going to steal all the prize noodles!

Ash, Misty, and Brock ran in front of the noodles, blocking Team Rocket's path.

"We aren't going let you steal these noodles!" Ash shouted. "Chikorita, go!" He threw a Poké Ball.

Chikorita popped out and landed on Ash's shoulder. The Grass Pokémon had a sleek, pale green body and four short legs. A long leaf grew from the top of its smooth head.

Chikorita nuzzled Ash affectionately.

"That's very nice," Ash said, embarrassed. "Now go get 'em!"

Chikorita jumped down to the ground.

"Toodles, noodles!" James shouted. He used the remote control to make the hot-air balloon lift up the supply of noodles.

"It's too late!" cried Brock with dismay.

"Chikorita!" countered Ash. "Use your Razor Leaf Attack."

Chikorita's sharp, boomerang-shaped leaves flew through the air and sliced the rope that attached the net to Team Rocket's balloon. The noodles fell to the ground.

"Give us those instant noodles this in-

stant!" James demanded. Then James released Weezing, his combination Poison and Gas Pokémon. Weezing looked like a purple cloud with two heads.

"Pikachu, use your Thundershock!" Ash commanded.

As Pikachu prepared to attack, Chikorita jealously bumped it out of the way. Pikachu went flying into one of the sunlight reflectors. The Pokémon's electric energy caused the mirror to shatter. The other reflectors burst apart in a chain reaction.

"No! Not the mirrors!" James cried.

With the light gone, the Sunfloras' heads shrunk back to their normal size.

"All right!" Sonrisa instructed Sonny. "You know what to do now, Sonny."

Sonny's petals lit up one by one, until its whole face was glowing. A shining beam radiated from Sonny.

"Is that —" said James fearfully.

"— what I think it is?" finished Jessie.

"It's using Solar Beam!" Meowth hissed.

The powerful attack slammed into Jessie,

James, and Meowth. The Pokémon thieves went sailing out of the town.

"Team Rocket's blasting off again!" they screamed.

"That was cool!" said Ash. He was in awe of the Sunflora's special power.

The crowd cheered wildly. The announcer picked up the microphone.

"The judges are ready to make their final decision," he said.

"Cyrus's Sunflora is excellent," remarked the first judge. "But Sonrisa's is simply extraordinary!"

"Sonrisa's Sunflora has such a sensational smile," added another judge.

"Just looking at it makes me feel so warm and happy!" agreed the other.

"The decision is unanimous, folks!" said the announcer. "Here are your winners of the Sunflora festival. Let's hear it for Sonrisa and her super-smiley Sunflora of the Year!"

Sonrisa smiled as she held up the golden trophy to the crowd. She thanked everyone, and then she and Sonny climbed down from the stage.

"Thank you so much," she told Ash and the others. "If it weren't for you, we never would have won the Sunflora of the Year award."

"You didn't win because of us, Sonrisa," Ash corrected her.

"It was all the hard work you put into training Sonny that won it," Misty told the girl with the sunny smile.

The friends spent the rest of the day celebrating at the festival. Early the next morning, they were back on the road. Ash was

sad to leave his new friend. But he was eager to get to the next town in the Johto Region. He, Brock, Misty, and Pikachu walked until they came to a beautiful valley in the middle of snow-covered mountains. They decided it was the perfect place to stop and have a picnic.

"Wow, what a view," Misty said as she took a deep breath of the mountain air. "And the weather's just perfect."

"This fresh air sure helps you work up an appetite," Brock remarked while chewing his sandwich.

"Mine doesn't need any help," Ash chuckled.

The friends were enjoying their picnic when they noticed a fluffy white Pokémon with a blue face and hooves. A little gold bell hung around the Pokémon's neck. Its black-and-yellow ears stuck out on each side of its head.

"What's that?" asked Misty.

"I think it's a Mareep," answered Brock.

Ash looked to Dexter for an explanation.

"Mareep, the Wool Pokémon," said the computer.

"Mareep store static electricity in their woolly coats. They are gentle, avoid battles and have mild dispositions."

"But Dexter didn't say how cute they are!" Misty giggled.

The Mareep came galloping toward the friends. It got close, closer, and then it didn't stop. It pounced right on top of Pikachu!

"This Mareep doesn't look too gentle to me!" Ash was worried.

Ash watched as the Mareep jumped all over Pikachu. Electricity flew out of Pikachu's cheeks. As it did, the Mareep's fur began to puff up. The Mareep was getting bigger and bigger!

"Pikachu!" Ash cried.

6

Mary Had a Little Mareep

Brock observed the fluffy Pokémon. "I see," he noted. "It collected Pikachu's electricity in its fleece."

"Like a hair dryer?" Misty asked curiously.

Suddenly, the friends heard the bleating of even more Mareep. A whole herd was coming down the hill. They were headed right for Pikachu!

Within seconds, the Mareep had surrounded Pikachu. The lightning Pokémon was caught in the middle of a herd of Mareep that were puffing up like popcorn.

"Look, now they're all getting puffed up!" Ash cried.

A little girl came running down the hill.

"Leave that Pikachu alone!" she shouted at the Mareep. "You all know better than to gang up on another Pokémon like that! Now stop it!"

The Mareep didn't listen.

"Leave that Pikachu alone!" the little girl demanded. "That electricity's not for you! Somebody is going to get hurt!"

The Mareep still didn't listen. In fact, they tossed the little girl right onto the ground.

"Are you okay?" Ash asked.

Before the girl could answer, Ash heard the voice of an older woman who was running toward them. "Mary!" she shouted.

"It's mommy!" the little girl informed them.

The little girl's mother had a Raichu with her. Raichu, the evolved form of Pikachu, was bigger than the yellow Pokémon, with more powerful electric attacks. Mary's mom instructed the orange Raichu to use its Thunderbolt attack. Streams of electricity shot out of the Raichu.

The Mareep ran toward the Raichu and pranced underneath the arc of power. The Raichu herded up all the Mareep.

"That's amazing!" observed Misty.

"It's almost like they're taking a static electricity shower," remarked Brock.

"Okay, Raichu, that will be enough," Mary's mom told the Pokémon. Then she turned to Ash and his friends.

"Let's get back to the house!" she said. With a wave of her hand, she invited Ash, Misty, Brock, and Pikachu to come along.

Ash was curious to find out more about the Mareep. As they walked, he watched in amazement as the Mareep obeyed Mary's mother's every command.

"I can't believe how obedient those Mareep are being!" said Misty as the Mareep headed in straight lines back to their corral.

When they were at the house, Mary's mother apologized to Ash.

"I'm sorry about what happened," she said. "Our Mareep love electricity so much they can't get enough."

"I understand," Ash said. "Besides, Pika-chu's okay. Aren't you, Pikachu?"

"Pika!" Pikachu smiled.

Ash sat back and took a sip of lemonade. Mary's mom had invited them to stay for a while. That sounded good to Ash. He was curious to find out more about those Ma-reep. And Mary and her mom were nice. They looked alike, except that Mary's brown hair was short, and her mom wore hers in a long ponytail.

Mary's mom turned to her daughter. "Something tells me you were daydreaming about Pokémon battles again."

Mary admitted she was daydreaming, even though she was supposed to be keep-ing her mind on herding the Mareep.

"But Mom, the festival starts next week!" Mary protested.

"What festival?" Ash asked. The Sunflora festival was so much fun. Were they lucky enough to stumble on another festival so quickly?

"For as long as anyone remembers the

Mareep in our valley have given us the best wool in the world, and so every —" Mary's mother didn't get to finish her sentence.

"Let me guess," Misty interrupted. "Every year you have a festival to honor the Mareep!" Ash knew she must have been thinking of the Sunflora festival, too.

"Right!" agreed Mary's mother. "It's an important part of our valley's history, and it's also lots of fun because we have events like Mareep judging and Pokémon battles."

Battles. That was just the word Ash was longing to hear.

"That's the event I'm going to enter and win!" he said excitedly.

Mary's mom explained that only people who live in the valley could enter the battles. Ash was disappointed. But Mary was excited to learn that Ash battled his Pokémon.

"I want to learn how to battle, too," said Mary longingly. She turned to her mother. "Mommy, can I enter the Mareep Festival Pokémon Battle?"

"You may not!" said her mother emphatically. "I've told you before you're too young!"

"No, I'm not!" Mary replied angrily.

"You're just not ready for battling yet," Mary's mom explained. "If you still have trouble handling your Mareep in the fields, how are you going to handle them in a battle?"

"But I —" Mary started.

"The festival is only five days away and you still have plenty of work to do," Mary's mother told her. "You need to stop dreaming about battling and concentrate on getting the Mareep ready for the contest."

The next day, Ash and the others helped Mary and her mother with the Mareep. Ash herded while Pikachu rode on one of the Mareep's back. Then Pikachu helped Raichu gather the Mareep by showering them with electricity. Brock helped Mary's mother record information about the wool Pokémon. Misty and Togepi brushed the fluffy Mareep's fleece.

When they were finished, Ash and Pikachu saw Mary secretly take one of the Mareep aside. They followed her. Mary commanded the Mareep to use its Thundershock Attack.

Bolts of electric energy shot out from the Pokémon and knocked into a stack of baled hay. The Mareep's aim was right on target.

"Did it learn that attack all by itself?" Ash asked.

Mary was startled. She thought she and her Mareep were alone.

"No, we've been practicing!" she informed Ash.

"Well, it shows," Ash complimented the little girl. "Do you have a name for this one?"

Mary introduced Ash to her Mareep,

Fluffy. Mary had raised Fluffy. They had been training together for a long time. Then Mary told Ash that she had a favor to ask him.

"Would you have a battle with me?" she asked shyly.

Ash was stunned. He didn't know how to answer.

Beating a little kid like Mary would be a piece of cake. He didn't want to make her feel bad.

"Please, Ash," Mary begged. "Fluffy and I were never in a Pokémon battle before."

Everyone has to start somewhere, he thought. He looked to Pikachu. "What do you say?" he asked.

"Pika," Pikachu nodded.

Ash told Mary that they would accept the challenge.

"I choose Fluffy!" Mary shouted.

Pikachu and Fluffy circled around each other.

"Fluffy, use Headbutt!" Mary commanded.

"Watch out, Pikachu!" warned Ash. But it was too late. The Mareep lowered its head and rammed into Pikachu, knocking the yellow Pokémon backward.

"Good work, Fluffy," cheered Mary. "Now use your Growl Attack!"

"Baaaaa," bleated the Mareep. The rumbling noise sent Pikachu flying.

"Fluffy, use Speed Star!" yelled Mary.

Small sparkling stars shot out of Mareep, zipped through the air and hit Pikachu.

Ash groaned.

It looked like he was going to lose a battle to a little kid!

7

Round Up

"Fluffy, Thundershock Attack!" commanded Mary. Blue bolts of electricity shot
from the Mareep.

"Pikachu, use your Thundershock, too!"
Ash countered.

Pikachu's bright yellow bolts met Fluffy's
blue bolts in midair. Both Pokémon struggled to gain the advantage. But they were
equally matched.

"Come on, Fluffy, don't give up!" Mary
pleaded.

"Pikachu, stop Thundershock!" Ash called unexpectedly.

Pikachu stopped the attack. It jumped out of the way of Fluffy's attack.

"Pika, pika," it squeaked.

"Just keep it up Fluffy," Mary told her Mareep. "We're winning!"

She couldn't understand why Ash had stopped Pikachu's attack. "Stronger now, turn up the power!" she commanded.

"Mary, no!" Ash tried to warn her, but it was too late. Mary had gone too far. Fluffy collapsed in a heap.

Ash and Mary rushed over to the weak Mareep.

"Fluffy, you have to get back up!" Mary begged.

"Fluffy used up all its energy in the attack," Ash explained. "Fluffy will be okay later after it has a good rest."

"Why did you stop Pikachu's Thundershock Attack?" Mary asked.

"Pikachu was getting all worn out," Ash informed her. "It was using its energy all afternoon watching the Mareep. If I had kept up with that electric attack, Pikachu would have been exhausted. I didn't want that to happen to my buddy."

"I never thought of that," Mary sighed. "I only thought about winning. Fluffy was doing such a great job and it looked like we were ahead. I thought I was just being tough like a Pokémon trainer should be."

Ash knew how Mary felt. When he had started training Pokémon, he didn't know a lot more than Mary. He only thought about winning, too. But then Ash saw that Pokémon battle because they like to win for their trainers. Now he knew that it was important for the trainers to care for their Pokémon as much as their Pokémon care for them.

Mary seemed to feel better after their talk. Together they walked back to the house, where Mary's mother had cooked a huge feast for them. After working hard all day, Ash was hungry. And tired. After dinner, they all fell into an exhausted sleep.

Sometime in the middle of the night, Mary's mom came in and lit a lantern in the bedroom. Ash could hear the wind howling outside.

"Is something the matter?" Brock asked sleepily.

"I'm so sorry to wake you all up," she answered, "but we really need your help right now."

Mary's mother led them all out into the stormy night.

"A good thunderstorm gives us a chance to get the Mareep in top condition by letting them take in lots of electricity. That helps their fleece look great and gets them all charged up for the festival," she explained.

Ash and the others followed Mary's mom outside. They were met with an amazing sight.

Raichu herded the Mareep and led them out onto a cliff. Lightning flashed. The bolts ripped through the sky and hit the herd of Mareep. Their fluffy fleece became even fluffier as the Mareep puffed up.

"Look at that!" Ash said as he pointed to the herd.

As the clouds parted, the Mareep's fleece shimmered in the darkness.

"Look at how pretty their fleece is," Misty noted. "It's all sparkly!"

The friends gazed at the beautiful Mareep. Suddenly, a net fell out of the sky onto the herd. They were trapped! The net rose up off the ground.

As Ash looked up, he saw a familiar sight. It was Team Rocket's Meowth-shaped hot-air balloon. And it was all lit up with colored lights!

"Isn't it way past your bedtime, twerp?" Jessie snarled.

"No, but it may be too late for you!" Ash answered. "Pikachu! Thunderbolt Attack!"

A steel arm shot out of Team Rocket's balloon before Pikachu could attack. It scooped up Pikachu and plopped the Pokémon into a wire cage. Now Team Rocket didn't just have all the Mareep. They had Pikachu, too!

8

Super Thundershock!

"We'll save you!" Ash called out to Pikachu. He would never let Team Rocket steal his Pokémon.

"Raichu, use your Thunderbolt!" Mary's mother yelled to her Electric Pokémon.

Raichu sent out a bolt that hit a silver panel on the balloon basket. The lights on the balloon glowed brighter.

"Raichu really hit the spot!" James sneered.

"Yes, the energy panel on our balloon helps brighten things up," Jessie added.

"Hurry, Raichu," Mary's mom commanded. "Maximum power!"

Raichu was determined. It focused all of its power on Team Rocket's balloon. Soon the energy panel exploded. The balloon went up in flames. It fell to the ground at the bottom of the cliff. The Mareep scrambled out of the burning balloon basket. Two Mareep scooted next to each other, and Pikachu's cage fell safely onto their soft, fluffy backs.

"It worked!" Ash cheered. But then he saw Raichu. The exhausted Pokémon had collapsed.

"Poor Raichu," Mary's mother said as she comforted the hardworking Pokémon. "I know that took everything out of you."

Ash and Mary ran down the hill to try to reach the Mareep. Ash could hear Mary's mother call to the Mareep from the top of the cliff. At her command, they grouped together.

"Use Thundershock!" Mary's mom finished.

Blue bolts of electricity sizzled through the air, aimed right at Team Rocket. But Meowth held up the broken energy panel. It re-

flected the Mareep's Thundershock Attack right back at them.

"Ash, they need a lot more power," Brock called to his friend. "They need Pikachu."

Ash ran to the cage. He picked up a rock and began banging on the metal lock.

Then Ash noticed that Fluffy was trying to get Mary's attention. Fluffy was trying to tell Mary something.

Mary understood. "Mommy, make the other Mareep aim their electricity into Fluffy!" she called out.

"It's worth a try," said Mary's mom. "All right, everyone. You heard what Mary said!"

The Mareep quickly obeyed. They sent all of their energy to Fluffy. As they did, Fluffy got bigger and bigger. Soon the Pokémon was enormous!

"Okay, Fluffy, use your Thundershock, now!" Mary commanded.

Fluffy now had the power of all the Mareep combined. Its Thundershock was incredible. Even the energy panel couldn't stop it.

"*Yow!*" Team Rocket wailed as the electric current surged through them.

While the Mareep attacked, Ash kept banging on the lock. Finally, the lock shattered. Pikachu sprang out, ready to battle.

"Finish them off, Pikachu!" Ash cried.

Sparks sizzled on Pikachu's red cheeks.

"Pikachuuuuuuu!" Pikachu cried, as it unleashed an enormous blast of electric energy.

Pikachu's Thunder Wave Attack sent Team Rocket over the edge. They blasted off once again. Ash raised his arms in victory.

"We did it!" Ash proclaimed.

"That was great, Fluffy," Mary hugged her Mareep.

Misty, Brock, and Mary's mom ran down to the bottom of the cliff. Mary's mother approached her. She took something out of her pocket and handed it to Mary.

"Mommy, that's a Poké Ball," Mary said. She was truly amazed.

"I think it's about time you had one," Mary's mother explained. "Grandma gave it to me when I was a girl. Maybe you can use it at the festival battle."

Mary smiled and hugged her mom.

"I can see you've learned a lot from our new friends," Mary's mom smiled. "I think you're ready to become a trainer now."

Ash was proud of Mary. But he knew he couldn't stay in the valley much longer. There were other Pokémon battles to fight — and probably other festivals.

9

What's a Wobbuffet?

A few days later, Ash and his friends found themselves on the boardwalk of a sunny beach.

"That breeze coming off the ocean sure feels good," Misty sighed as the wind touched her face.

The friends heard a strange voice coming from the boardwalk. Ash turned to look. A boy with black hair and a striped shirt was talking to a big blue Pokémon.

"Keep your back nice and straight," said

the boy. "Stand tall so people can see that you're a great Pokémon."

The Pokémon blinked its narrow eyes. It had a bullet-shaped body, long arms, and a dark tail that dragged on the ground.

Ash took out Dexter.

"What is that strange-looking Pokémon?" he asked.

"Wobbuffet, the patient Pokémon," said Dexter. "It chooses to live in dark areas in order to hide its pitch-black tail."

"Wobbuffet, huh?" Ash said. "I'd like to find out more about this Pokémon." He introduced himself and his friends to the boy.

"My name's Benny," the boy replied.

"What were you doing?" asked Ash.

"I'm getting my Wobbuffet in shape for the Pokémon swap meet."

"The Pokémon swap meet?" questioned Ash. "What's that?"

"It's a huge festival held in Leaf Town," Benny explained. "Pokémon trainers trade their Pokémon with other trainers."

Ash chuckled. "A trading festival."

"That sounds great," added Brock.

"I don't know, Benny," Misty said as she looked at the Wobbuffet. "I wouldn't get my heart set on trading *this* Pokémon if I were you."

"Misty!" Brock scolded.

"I mean, it sure is charming when you look carefully," Misty corrected herself.

Benny sighed. "I know Wobbuffet is weird," he said. "Don't get me wrong. I love it. But I'd like to try raising other Pokémon, too."

Ash understood. He hated to lose any of his Pokémon. But sometimes it was the best thing for both the Pokémon and the trainer.

"I'm sure you'll find the perfect Pokémon

for you at the swap meet," Ash said. "Can we come with you?"

"Sure!" said Benny. He seemed cheered up by the thought of having someone to talk to besides Wobbuffet.

The friends followed Benny through the streets of Leaf Town. Suddenly, people came running at them from all directions. Ash stopped. A strange rumbling noise was getting closer and closer.

Ash gasped. Hundreds of Tauros were stampeding behind the people. The wild bull Pokémon were big and strong, and had pointy horns.

Ash picked up Pikachu and ran for cover.

"We'd better move!" he yelled to his friends. "The Tauros are headed this way!"

10

Good-bye, Heracross, Hello Tauros!

Ash and his friends quickly reached the safety of the sidewalk. The Tauros thundered down the street.

"What's going on?" Brock wondered out loud.

A man stopped to explain. "It's the running of the Tauros. This town is famous for it. The Tauros run down the street. If you're brave enough, you can try to step in the street and touch a Tauros horn."

The man jumped in front of the stampeding herd.

Now Ash was excited. He loved a new challenge. "I'm going to try, too!" he cried.

"Be careful, Ash!" warned Misty.

Ash ran out in front of the herd. The sight of the stampeding Tauros was overwhelming. He stood there as long as he could, but jumped out of the way at the last minute. He didn't have a chance to touch a Tauros's horn.

"It's harder than it looks," Benny said.

"I'm confused," Misty said. "Where's the swap meet?"

"That will start soon," Teru said. "The running of the Tauros is just one of the events leading up to the swap meet. Now trainers will battle their Tauros in the stadium."

"That's something I've got to see," Ash said. He had captured a herd of Tauros once, in the safari zone. He liked battling with his Tauros, but he could only carry six Poké Balls at a time. Right now his herd of Tauros was under the care of Professor Oak, back in Ash's hometown.

Benny led Ash and the others to the

round, open-air arena. They stood in the stands, watching two trainers pit their Tauros against each other.

"I can't just watch," Ash said as the urge to compete came over him. "I've got to get into battle now!"

Ash couldn't wait to get his Tauros and join the battle. He headed for the Pokémon Center so he could get in touch with Professor Oak. He called the professor on the videophone and told him about the Tauros battles.

"That's fine, Ash," Professor Oak said. "You already have six Pokémon with you. You'll have to send one back to me before I can send you your Tauros."

It was a tough decision, but Ash chose Heracross, a Bug Pokémon he had captured early in his Johto journey. He put Heracross's Poké Ball into the transporter machine. In an instant he was holding Tauros's Poké Ball. He was ready to compete!

Ash headed back to the stadium and signed up for the battle. Soon he faced Fernando, the most successful Tauros trainer in Leaf Town.

"I'm Ash from Pallet Town," Ash said as an introduction. "I challenge you to a Tauros battle."

"All right, bring it on," answered Fernando.

Ash and Fernando each threw a Poké Ball in the air at the same time. The two Tauros appeared in a blaze of light. Ash's Tauros lowered its head and snorted. Its three long tails waved back and forth.

"Tauros, Take Down!" commanded Ash.

"You, too. Take Down!" Fernando countered.

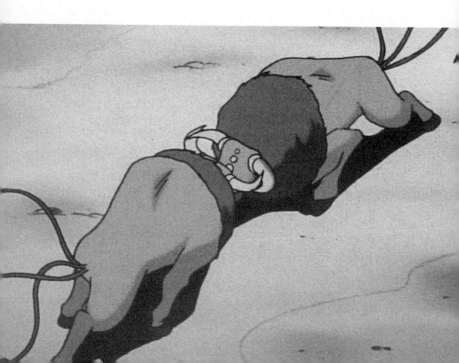

The two Tauros locked horns. They were both strong.

"Good job, Tauros," Fernando cheered. "Keep pushing."

"Don't give in Tauros!" Ash shouted. "Take Down!"

The Tauros battled back and forth. But Ash's Tauros was stronger. Soon Ash's Tauros sent Fernando's Tauros flying!

"All right!" Ash cheered. It always felt great to do well against a seasoned trainer.

Ash's friends cheered him when he got back to the stands.

"What do you say we check out the swap meet?" Benny asked. "I'd like to see what I can get for my Wobbuffet."

"Sounds good to me," Ash said. Benny led them to the town square. Crowds of Pokémon trainers milled around, showing off their Pokémon as they looked to make a trade.

Ash recognized the Pokémon exchange machines. A screen rose up from a tabletop. A tube-shaped arm extended from each side of the screen. When trainers decided to

73

trade, they each placed their Poké Ball under one arm. The tubes sucked up the Poké Balls and the Pokémon inside switched balls. Then the newly filled Poké Balls were dropped back onto the tabletop. The whole process could be viewed on the screen.

As Ash walked around the festival, he found that he was very popular in Leaf Town. He was soon surrounded by other trainers. Everyone wanted to talk to the trainer who had beaten Fernando.

"Trade me for this Onix," pleaded one trainer.

"Hold on," stopped another. "What about my Nidoqueen?

"I'll trade you my Rhyhorn," begged another.

"Whoa," Ash told them. "Sorry, but I'm not trading my Tauros."

It seemed as if everyone wanted to trade for Ash's Tauros, but Benny couldn't find a taker for his Wobbuffet anywhere.

"Hey Benny! Looks like you haven't found anybody to trade with yet." Ash said.

"Not so far, but I know I will sooner or later," Benny answered dejectedly.

"There are so many people and so many Pokémon here," Brock said. "There's got to be *one* trainer who'd like to swap with you."

"Let's all look," suggested Misty. They all set out to find a trainer to trade Pokémon with Benny.

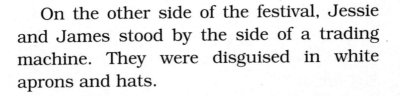

On the other side of the festival, Jessie and James stood by the side of a trading machine. They were disguised in white aprons and hats.

"Step right up, everyone," Jessie called to the crowd. "See the most up-to-date Poké-Exchange Machine."

"Not only does it provide super swift swapping, but as an extra added bonus it raises the level of each Pokémon in the process," James added.

Trainers fought to get a turn trading on the new machine. Team Rocket couldn't make trades fast enough.

Meowth lounged in a pile of Poké Balls behind the machine. "This exchange machine is a complete fake," it purred. "We keep the Pokémon and give the Poké Balls back empty!"

Team Rocket's machine was the most popular trading site at the festival.

"This plan is our best yet," Jessie whispered to James. "Soon we'll have every Pokémon in Leaf Town!"

11

Swap Meet Scam

Ash and his friends didn't know anything about Team Rocket's plot. They wandered around the festival trying to help Benny.

"There must be somebody around here who'd like to trade for a Wobbuffet," Misty said. As she spoke, Psyduck popped out of its Poké Ball. It stuck its head out of Misty's backpack.

"I suggest you stay inside your Poké Ball, Psyduck," Misty chided her Psychic Pokémon. "You might give *me* ideas about trading."

A crowd of trainers surrounded Misty.

"Hey, a Psyduck!" yelled one boy.

"That one's cool!" said a girl.

"You really think this Psyduck is cool?" Misty asked. She couldn't believe what she was hearing.

"I just love that empty look on its face," said another trainer.

"Trade it for my Marill," begged one boy.

"No, for my Oddish," demanded another girl.

"I'll trade you my Stantler!" offered one trainer.

"No, take my Mareep!" demanded another.

"No!" was Misty's final answer. "I won't trade my Psyduck!" She looked at the pesky Pokémon. "Maybe you're worth something after all, Psyduck."

Ash approached a girl trainer. She held a furry brown Pokémon with a long, striped tail. "Would you trade your Sentret for a Wobbuffet?" he asked.

"I'll pass," said the girl, as she looked at the Wobbuffet. The Pokémon had a blank expression on its face.

"I guess it's hopeless," Benny moped.

"That's a great Stantler you have there," Brock said to another trainer, admiring its beautiful antlers.

"I worked hard to raise it," replied the trainer.

"Would you consider trading it for a Wob-buffet?" Brock asked.

"It's one of the best Wobbuffet you'll ever see," Ash chimed in.

"Raising Pokémon like this is part of the thrill of being a trainer," continued Brock.

"And this one is really obedient, a good Pokémon," Ash said as he poured on the charm.

The boy could hardly resist. "Why not?" he replied. "Let's trade."

Ash, Brock, and Benny had finally found a taker! They rushed to find an exchange machine. They stopped at the first one they could find — the one belonging to Jessie and James.

Ash didn't suspect anything. Benny placed his Poké Ball on the machine. The other trainer started to do the same, but stopped.

"I changed my mind," he told Benny. "I really want a Flying Pokémon. Maybe another time." He took his Poké Ball and walked away.

While Benny sulked, Jessie was being jostled. James bumped into Jessie. One of her Poké Balls accidentally fell on the machine that held Benny's Poké Ball. Before Jessie noticed, the Pokémon were traded.

Benny didn't notice, either. He picked up his Poké Ball and glumly tucked it into his pocket.

Ash studied the two clumsy people who ran the trading machine. There was something familiar about them.

Suddenly, a swell of angry voices filled the air.

"Those guys are fakes!"

"They're thieves! Our Poké Balls are empty!"

A crowd of Pokémon trainers surrounded the trading machine.

Fakes? Thieves? That could only mean one thing.

"Team Rocket!" Ash cried.

Misty and Brock figured it out, too.

"What mischief are you up to now?" asked Misty.

Jessie and James whipped off their white aprons and hats. "That's right. We did it," Jessie said. "We used a fake exchange machine to exchange *full* Poké Balls for *empty* ones. Pretty smart planning, wouldn't you say?"

Ash didn't agree. "Give everyone back their Pokémon!" he demanded.

Team Rocket looked at the crowd and laughed. Meowth took out a device that looked like a vacuum-cleaner attachment.

"We're not giving back anything," screeched Meowth.

A rope shot out of the device and wrapped around the crowd. Everyone was all tied up!

"We'd love to talk this over with you but you're obviously a little *tied up* at the moment," Meowth chuckled.

Ash struggled against the tight rope. There was no way out.

"We're in trouble now," Ash said with dismay.

12

Tauros, Take Down!

"Now suck up the rest of their Pokémon" ordered Jessie.

James took out a giant vacuum. A huge suction hit the crowd. Poké Balls went flying out of trainer's pockets and into James's vacuum.

"Ash!" Misty cried.

Ash had to think of a plan fast. Then he remembered his first experience in Leaf Town — the running of the Tauros.

"That's it! Tauros!" he said to himself.

"Everybody, release your Tauros," he called to the crowd.

The trainers took out their Poké Balls and held them up in the air. Soon a crowd of Tauros filled the town square. The trainers shouted their commands at once.

"Take Down!" they yelled.

The herd of Tauros thundered toward Team Rocket. They slammed into Jessie, James, and Meowth with their horns. That was all it took to send Team Rocket flying right into their hot-air balloon. The air poured out of the balloon and sent it sailing into the distance. A sack full of Poké Balls fell into the crowd.

One trainer released his Scyther.

"Cut the rope, Scyther," the trainer ordered. The Scyther used its sharp bladelike wings to cut the rope and release the crowd.

After the trainers were set free, they rushed to get their Poké Balls back. But what they got was a surprise.

"They tricked us," one trainer informed the crowd. "These are all fake Poké Balls."

Team Rocket had filled the balloon with

fake Poké Balls. They dropped them on purpose to distract the trainers.

Ash and his friends didn't need to hear any more. They were already running.

"All right!" shouted Ash. "Let's go get those Pokémon back!"

It didn't take Ash long to find Team Rocket. They were trying to fix their battered balloon.

"Give back everybody's Poké Balls," Ash demanded. "Chikorita, I choose you!" cried Ash.

Jessie threw a Poké Ball, too. But it wasn't the Pokémon she expected.

"I didn't know Team Rocket had a Wobbuffet," commented Ash.

Jessie was shocked.

"Oh, no!" she said. "I must have traded one of my Pokémon by accident. How else would I end up with this pathetic Pokémon?"

"*Wobbuffet,*" the Pokémon said in a high, scratchy voice.

Jessie sighed. "Let's see what this blue buffoon can do," she said. "Wobbuffet, attack them!"

"*Wobbuffet.*" The Pokémon didn't move a muscle.

James leafed through a Pokémon guidebook.

"Let's see. This says that Wobbuffett is called the Patient Pokémon. It can't attack," James relayed.

"What does Team Rocket need with a Pokémon that doesn't attack?" Jessie howled.

Ash saw that Team Rocket was confused. He knew the time was right to get back everyone's Poké Balls.

"Chikorita, Vine Whip," he called out.

Chikorita's long vines shot out at Wobbuffet. Wobbuffet didn't even blink. But its body glowed with a faint red light. The attack hit the light and bounced right back at Chikorita.

"It sure does seem to be a patient Poké-mon," noticed Meowth.

"But that doesn't do us any good at all," whined Jessie. "Doesn't Wobbuffet know any attacks?" Jessie grabbed the guidebook from James.

"Chikorita, use Vine Whip once more," ordered Ash.

"Let's try this," Jessie said. "Wobbuffet, Counter!"

Once again, Chikorita's attack bounced right off Wobbuffet and came back to Chikorita.

"Don't give in, Chikorita," Ash encouraged his Pokémon. "Razor Leaf!" Chikorita shot sharp leaves straight at Wobbuffet.

"Wobbuffet! Use Counter once more," Jessie replied. Every Razor Leaf went flying back to Chikorita. The little Grass Pokémon squealed and dodged the sharp leaves.

"I never knew Wobbuffet's Counter was that strong," observed Brock.

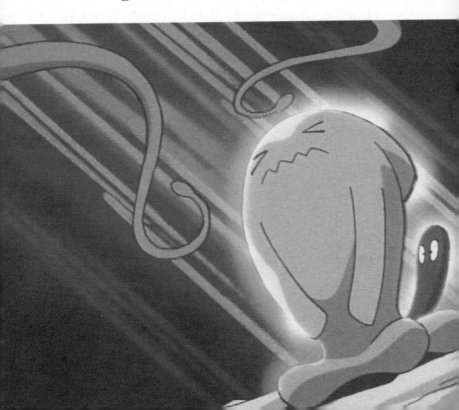

Ash had to order Chikorita to return. There was nothing it could do against Wobbuffet.

"Help me out, Pikachu," Ash asked his Pokémon.

"Pika pika," answered Pikachu.

"Pikachu, Thunderbolt!" Ash commanded.

Pikachu hurled a sizzling lightning bolt at Wobbuffet. Once again, Jessie's Pokémon started to glow a soft red.

Bam! The bolt knocked into Wobbuffet. But this time, it bounced back — and knocked into Team Rocket.

Jessie, James, Meowth, and Wobbuffet flew over the horizon. "Looks like we're blasting off again!" they cried.

Ash and the others gathered up the real Poké Balls and carried them back to the town square. A rush of trainers surrounded them, eager to get back their Pokémon.

"Hey Ash," Benny called. He was standing with a Lickitung. The pudgy pink Pokémon came up to Benny's shoulder. It licked Benny's cheek with its long, sticky tongue.

Ash recognized it right away. Jessie had a

Lickitung. She must have traded it for Wob-buffet by mistake.

"I wanted to thank the girl in white who traded with me," said Benny. "Have you seen her anywhere?"

Ash chuckled. "I sure haven't."

"I wanted to ask her to take good care of Wobbuffet," Benny added sadly.

He called out into the sunset. "Lady, my Wobbuffet is very, very kind, so please treat it nicely, okay? Bye-bye Wobbuffet. Take care." Tears streamed down Benny's face.

"I wonder if I'd cry, too, if Psyduck and I went separate ways," Misty remarked.

"It's hard to say good-bye to one of your own Pokémon, no matter who you are," Brock sighed.

Ash knew just how Benny felt. As Ash journeyed from place to place, he always made new friends. Then he always had to say good-bye to them. Sometimes he even had to say good-bye to a Pokémon. It wasn't easy. But there was one thing Ash would never say good-bye to. He would never say

good-bye to his dream to become the world's greatest Pokémon trainer.

"Good-bye," Ash called as he left Leaf Town.

Good-bye to festivals. Good-bye to good new friends.

"Hello to a brand-new adventure," Ash thought as he headed down the road.

About the Author

Sheila Sweeny loves writing books almost as much as she loves reading them. She also enjoys playing hockey and watching almost every other sport. But lately her favorite way to spend time is to play with her new baby, Jake. She likes Meowth a lot because it reminds her of her cat, Kovalev. They are both always in trouble. Sheila grew up in Brooklyn, New York, and still lives there with her family.